W9-BMV-349

TOM
AND
HUCK

A Novel by Liz Fox

Based on the motion picture from Walt Disney Pictures
Based on the novel *The Adventures of Tom Sawyer* by Mark Twain
Screenplay by Stephen Sommers and David Loughery
Produced by Laurence Mark and John Baldecchi
Directed by Peter Hewitt

114 Fifth Avenue
New York, NY 10011-5690

First Disney Press Paperback Edition 1995

For information address Disney Press, 114 Fifth Avenue, New York, New York 10011-5690.

PRINTED IN THE UNITED STATES OF AMERICA.

1 3 5 7 9 10 8 6 4 2

This book is set in 12-point Minister Book.
Designed by Lara S. Demberg.

Library of Congress Catalog Card Number: 95-74736

ISBN: 0-7868-4064-1

contents

one
Murderous Intentions

A cold April rain whipped the empty streets of Hannibal. Thunder rumbled and dark clouds scudded across the moon. A lone figure glided silently down the streets.

He stopped under a creaking sign that announced, "Dr. J.R. Robinson, Undertaker and Taxidermist," then slipped past a row of rough wood coffins, and through the door.

◆ ◆ ◆

In a candlelit room, a tall gloomy man hovered over a neatly dressed corpse laid out on a slab. It was hard to say who was more deathlike—the corpse or the undertaker. Doc Robinson was as gaunt and cadaverous as any corpse he had ever embalmed.

"Smile, will you?" Doc Robinson tried vainly to prod the corpse's face into a smile. His customers expected a peaceful, contented look on their dearly departed.

Suddenly, the door swung open. A gust of wind blew out most of the candles. Into the darkened room stepped a tall, powerful-looking man, with long black hair and fierce cold eyes.

Doc Robinson glared at Injun Joe. "Shut the door . . ."

Injun Joe's eyes narrowed with anger. No one in Hannibal—or anywhere else—ordered him around. If they did, they lived to regret it.

"I have a job for you," Doc Robinson said.

"What kind of job?" His tone was surly.

"It's heavy work, we'll need another man."

A suspicious look crossed Injun Joe's face. "When do you want it done?"

"Soon." The undertaker didn't trust Injun Joe, but there weren't many men he could ask to do *this* job.

"Where?"

"The graveyard."

Injun Joe raised an eyebrow.

"Unless you're afraid," Doc Robinson said curtly. He turned back to the corpse. "The job pays two dollars. Take it or leave it."

Casually, Injun Joe pulled a long knife from inside his coat. "I'll take it." He paused meaningfully. "But the job pays three dollars."

He slowly wiped the blade of his knife on Doc Robinson's chest. "Unless you think I deserve more."

"No, no," Doc Robinson babbled in terror. "Three dollars sounds fair."

Injun Joe fixed Doc Robinson with his cold, malevolent stare. Then he turned and strode out of the room, slamming the door behind him. The remaining candles guttered and extinguished, leaving the undertaker in darkness.

The clock chimed, giving Doc Robinson's shattered nerves another fright. It was midnight.

two
Capsized

As the clock struck midnight at Doc Robinson's, Tom Sawyer threw off the bedcovers and jumped out of bed fully dressed. He glanced at the bed next to him. His too-good-to-be-true cousin Sidney snored peacefully. Good thing. He didn't want that sneaky little tattletale ruining his carefully laid plans with Ben and Joe.

Holding the bedsheet, Tom tiptoed over to the window, quietly raised the sash, and flung one leg over the sill.

"And where do you think you're going?" It was

Sid, sitting up in bed, his arms folded across his chest, smiling smugly.

"Go back to sleep, Sid," Tom said airily. "I'm just runnin' away from home."

"Again?"

"This time for good." Tom couldn't contain his excitement. "Me and Joe Harper and Ben Rogers is goin' to New Orleans to be steamboat men."

"Not if I tell Aunt Polly!" Sid crowed triumphantly. He opened his mouth to yell for her. But Tom was too quick for him. He jumped on Sid, pushed him back onto his pillow, and clamped a strong hand over his mouth.

"I had a feelin' you was gonna be your usual nasty self so I rigged up a little surprise." Tom reached under the bed, pulled out a dirty sock, and stuffed it into Sid's mouth.

With a flourish, he brought out a topless glass jar, which he balanced on Sid's chest. "Just so you won't be lonely . . ."

Sid's eyes bulged with terror when he saw what was in the jar.

"That's a black widow, Sid," Tom said. "The most poisonous spider in the whole world. You knock over that jar and she's gonna be mad."

As Sid lay paralyzed with fear, Tom sauntered to the window and picked up the bedsheet. "Course I could be wrong. It might just be a harmless fruit spider. But there's only one way to find out . . ." With a final triumphant grin at his cousin, he slipped out of the window, into the darkness.

◆ ◆ ◆

Running as fast as he could, Tom raced through the back alleys of Hannibal. There was Joe Harper, right on schedule, jumping silently down from a tree to join him. Then Ben Rogers leaped over a fence. Their group was complete.

The three boys raced past dark storefronts down Main Street. Zooming around a corner, they almost collided with Muff Potter.

"Hey, Muff!" Tom cried in delight.

"Howdy, boys. Where ya headed this time of night?" Muff drank too much, but he had a good heart and was a friend to all the boys in Hannibal.

"We're running away from home," Tom told him.

"Oh, I used to do that all the time," Muff said. "'Til home ran away from me. Came back one day and everybody was gone."

"Where'd they go?" Joe looked a little scared.

"As far away as they could." Muff laughed.

Ben and Joe exchanged anxious looks. What if their families decided to run away from *them*?

"Come on," Tom said impatiently. He wasn't worried about anything. He wanted to be off on the adventure.

As the boys took off, Muff called after them. "Hey! When ya comin' back?"

"Never!" Tom cried.

As they disappeared, Muff said softly to himself, "See ya tomorrow."

◆ ◆ ◆

The three boys clambered down a steep wooded bank. Hidden by a thick tangle of bushes and trees was their own secret harbor where an anchored log raft awaited them. Moonlight shone over the boat and the water, making strange rippling patterns.

Silently the three boys boarded their craft and raised the anchor. Tom tied on his bedsheet for a sail. Then they cast off the lines, lit a lamp, and hung it from the mast.

For a moment, Ben and Joe gazed sadly at the town.

"Don't tell me you're gettin' homesick

already," Tom said. "We haven't even left!"

"No, Tom." Ben looked down. "It's just—well, ain't you gonna miss your family?"

Tom sighed with exasperation. "You think steamboat men got families? Heck, that's the main reason we're runnin' away, ain't it? So's we can be free to do what we want—when we want—and not have to answer to anybody."

He grabbed their things and started piling them on the side of the raft. "If you boys want to go home . . ."

Ben hesitated, then shook his head. "No, Tom. We made a pact."

"Last chance," Tom warned them. "Once we push off there's no turning back."

Joe and Ben exchanged glances. "No, Tom," said Joe. "We're with ya. All the way."

◆ ◆ ◆

The wind took hold of the sail and the raft began to move downstream. "Goodbye, Hannibal!"

The raft picked up speed. "Luff, and bring her to the wind."

"Aye, aye, sir!"

Water came crashing over the bow, spraying the boys. "Next stop, New Orleans!" Tom cried. "Nothin' can stop us now."

As the raft spun down the creek, the water became rougher and rougher. The raft plunged and dove giddily. Tom was worried but tried to hide it from his friends. The boys tried hard to keep the raft steady.

Suddenly a huge mass of rock and thorny branches rose up before them.

"Joe! Hard to port!" Tom screamed.

It was too late. The raft smashed onto the rocks, throwing Tom forward into the mast where he banged his head. Joe and Ben tumbled into the rushing water.

"Tom!" Joe yelled, terrified.

There was no reply. The raft did another somersault over the rocks and smashed back into the water. Tom had slumped unconscious to the base of the mast. Gasping for breath, his two friends struggled to shore.

Tom and the raft sank deeper into the water.

Out of nowhere a dark figure appeared in the raging creek and pulled Tom out. He dragged Tom's limp body to shore and gently placed him on the bank. Two filthy hands pumped his chest until Tom began to sputter and cough.

Tom's eyes flickered open. He saw a strange face silhouetted against the night sky. His mysterious rescuer looked at him for a long moment; then he disappeared.

Tom sat up, dazed, as Joe and Ben arrived. Their faces showed their relief at finding Tom.

three
Whitewashin'

Later, the three bedraggled boys shuffled into town. Tom shimmied up the drainpipe of Aunt Polly's house and climbed through the open window of his room. The room was empty. Sid's bed was, of course, neatly made. Tom grabbed a pile of newspapers he kept under his bed and changed into clean clothes. Then he went downstairs to greet Aunt Polly, Sid, and his sixteen-year-old cousin, Mary, in the kitchen.

"Mornin', everybody," he said cheerfully as if he had slept in his bed all night. "What's for breakfast?"

"You can start with this," Aunt Polly snapped. She banged the jar containing the spider on the table.

"Couldn't I just have some scrambled eggs?"

Aunt Polly jumped up and grabbed Tom by the collar. "I've a notion to skin you alive. Sneaking out 'til all hours, worrying a body to death . . ."

At the table, Sid grinned.

"Shall I get the switch?" Tom turned toward the back door. He had known this was coming and he was ready for it. He had already lined the back of his pants with the newspapers.

"No." Aunt Polly sat back down in her chair. "I'll just be obliged to make you work tomorrow."

"Tomorrow?" Tom couldn't keep the disappointment out of his voice. "Couldn't I take a whipping?"

Aunt Polly shook her head. "I've got to do *something* and I ain't got the heart to hit you."

"But tomorrow's Saturday . . ." he pleaded.

"I've got to do some of my duty by you, now sit!"

Tom reached behind him and pulled out the wad of newspapers from inside his pants. He would have to work after all. With a disappointed sigh, he sat down in his chair.

◆ ◆ ◆

Tom stepped through the gate, carrying a bucket of whitewash and a long-handled brush. With a practiced eye, he surveyed the fence that he had to paint. It was a monster: thirty yards long, nine feet high. He was going to be old by the time this was done.

"Buffalo gals, won't you come out tonight . . ." piped a small thin voice.

Tom stopped in his tracks. He stared at the little boy carrying an empty water bucket. An idea had just occurred to him.

"Hello, Jim, ol' buddy."

"Hello, Tom," Jim said warily.

"Tell ya what. I'll go to the pump for you if you'll whitewash some."

"Can't do it. Old Missus said she'd tar the head off of me if I let you talk me into white-washin'."

"You ain't afraid of her, are you?" Tom said incredulously.

His eyes widening in fear, Jim nodded. "Good-bye, Tom." He began to walk away.

"I'll show you my bloody toe!" Tom called after him.

It was a tempting offer. Jim stopped.

"It's got pus!"

The small boy dropped his bucket.

"Yellow—dripping—pus," Tom finished.

Jim spun around. "You got a deal!" he cried.

As he leaned over to get a closer look, a broom swatted him hard on the rear. Jim yelped, grabbed his bucket, and dashed down the road.

Broom in hand, Aunt Polly towered over Tom. She pointed to the fence. "No excuses!" she said sternly.

Tom frowned. Now there was no way out. Reluctantly he picked up his brush, dipped it in the whitewash, and began to paint.

He had barely begun when Billy Newton, another small neighborhood boy, came up the lane, pretending to be a steamboat.

A slow smile spread across Tom's face. There *was* a solution to his problems. He dipped his brush in the whitewash bucket again and pretended to paint with great enthusiasm.

Billy came over to watch, a puzzled expression on his face. Everyone in Hannibal knew Tom Sawyer hated work. "You feelin' okay, Tom?"

"Oh, hi, Billy." Tom feigned surprise. "I was having so much fun I didn't hear you comin'."

"Fun?"

"Whitewashin' this here fence." Tom whistled a happy tune.

"That ain't fun," Billy said. "That's work."

"Well, maybe it is, and maybe it ain't. All I know is, it suits Tom Sawyer." He slapped some more paint on the fence and continued to whistle. He even exclaimed that a boy doesn't get a chance to whitewash a fence every day.

"Say, Tom," Billy said shyly. "Let me white-wash a little."

Tom frowned and shook his head. "Aunt Polly's awful peculiar about this fence."

"Just a little?" Billy pleaded.

"Billy, I'd like to, but Aunt Polly—well, Jim wanted to do it, but she wouldn't let him. If you was to tackle this fence and anything was to happen to it . . ."

"I'd be real careful," Billy promised.

"What'll you give me?" Tom asked.

◆ ◆ ◆

Tom sat under a tree, reading *Robin Hood* and fingering his new black cat's-eye marble, while Billy and half a dozen other small boys finished whitewashing the fence. In front of him were heaped a brass doorknob, some tadpoles in a jar, candy, a kite, and some firecrackers—his "fees" for whitewashing the fence.

Looking lazily up from his book, Tom saw Ben and Joe coming up the lane. "Well, if it ain't the two bravest steamboat men on the Mississippi," he said sarcastically.

"Lookit, Tom, we're awfully sorry about last night not workin' out," Ben apologized.

Joe stepped forward. "We could build another boat."

Tom waved them away. "Forget it. Anybody can be a steamboat man these days. But outlaws—that's somethin' else."

"Outlaws?" Joe's eyes flickered with interest.

Tom held up the book. "Sure. Like Robin Hood and his Merry Men. All we need is the woods and some bows and arrows. We'll rob from the rich and give to the poor! We'll—"

He stopped abruptly. A sleek black carriage was rolling down the lane. The whitewashers had all stopped painting to stare at it. "It's the new judge," someone whispered.

Judge Thatcher, a distinguished man with silvery hair, held the reins, while on the seat next to him, his twelve-year-old daughter, Becky, nibbled on an apple.

The book fell from Tom's hand and all thoughts of Robin Hood vanished. He had never seen anyone as pretty as Becky Thatcher.

Bump! Becky's apple went flying out of her hand. The three boys scrambled for it. Joe snatched it up, while Tom tried frantically to grab it from him. But Joe and Ben tossed the apple back and forth, keeping it tantalizingly over Tom's head.

"What'll you take for it?" Tom was desperate. He *had* to have that apple.

"What'll you give?" Ben countered.

Tom motioned to his pile of new treasures. "Everything."

Their mouths dropped open. They tossed him the apple and raced to the pile.

With the precious apple in his hand, Tom ran after the carriage. Maybe he could give it back to her. Becky would be grateful. She would smile at him. She would remember him . . .

As he hurtled around a corner, a foot flew out and tripped him. Tom sprawled on the ground and the apple flew from his hand into Huck Finn's.

"Thanks." Huck polished the apple on his tattered jacket and took a bite.

Tom jumped to his feet. "Huck! You're back! Where've you been? What've you been doing?"

Huck shrugged and took another bite of the apple. He was taller than Tom, harder and more muscular. "I'm a traveler. I go to lots of places. Upriver, downriver. Bound to pass through here sometime."

Tom stared at him for a long moment. "You're the one who pulled me out the other night," he said slowly.

"I felt like a swim." Huck shrugged the rescue off. "Come on, I'll show you my place."

The boys made their way out of town. Huck's home was outdoors, nestled between rocks, which made a kind of natural room. Old, cast-off furniture was scattered around. A hammock hung between a tree and rock. There were chipped ornaments, cups and pots, and a barrel mounted high in the tree as a lookout.

Tom thought he had never seen any place so wonderful. "How long you been living here, Huck?"

Huck took a seat on a tall thronelike rock. "About a month."

"A month, huh?" A small smile crept across Tom's face. "Last week, Aunt Polly whupped me for swipin' a pie coolin' on the windowsill. But it wasn't me. I figured it was Sid."

"He wanted it," Huck said. "But I beat him to it."

"I oughta punch you in the nose," Tom said, half joking.

Huck spun around. "You're welcome to try." There was an edge of danger in his voice.

Tom backed away. He wasn't going to mess with Huck. He was a friend—and a fierce fighter, too. "Maybe later."

Huck shrugged and climbed up to his barrel lookout.

"So, when you're not stealin' food, or saving folks from drowning, what do you do all day?" Tom called up to him.

"Whatever I want," Huck said.

Tom sat down on Huck's throne and gazed at him with envy and a little awe. "You're lucky."

"Yep—I'm a free man," Huck bragged. "I do what I want when I want to do it. And I go where I want when I want to go there."

He climbed down from his crow's nest and motioned to Tom to get off his throne. Tom stepped off with a smile. "I'm glad you came back, Huck," he said. "It's good to see you."

"It is?" Huck seemed suddenly uncomfortable.

Tom held out his hand.

"What's that for?" Huck asked suspiciously.

"It's what friends do."

"Your old Auntie catches you with me, she'll whip you from here to St. Louis."

"This is nothing to do with her," Tom said firmly. "We were friends before. Don't you remember?"

"Yeah, I guess we were," Huck admitted.

"Well, we're friends again."

"Yeah, I guess we are." Huck awkwardly extended his hand and the two boys shook on their friendship.

four

Becky and the Red Apple

With a plan in mind, Tom strolled up the walk to school, tossing a shiny new red apple into the air.

Shoving the apple into his pocket, he sauntered into the classroom, where the girls sat on one side and the boys on the other. School had already begun.

"Thomas Sawyer!" Schoolmaster Dobbins glared at him.

Tom tried to look remorseful. "Sorry I'm late, Mr. Dobbins."

"Well? What's your excuse this time?"

Tom glanced over at Becky. There was an

empty chair right next to her. And he was going to sit in it. "I stopped to talk with Huckleberry Finn," he announced.

The room was shocked into silence. Huck was an outcast, a pariah. Every mother in the town kept her children away from him.

"Thomas Sawyer, this is the most astounding confession I have ever listened to!" Mr. Dobbins sputtered. "You are not unaware that it is forbidden to associate with that idle wastrel?"

"No, sir—I mean, yes, sir."

"Then you must realize that I shall have to punish you."

"You want me to go to the whipping post?" Tom offered.

"No, whipping's too good for you. I shall have to think of something more humiliating."

Tom feigned horror. "Please, Mr. Dobbins, you're not gonna make me sit with the girls!"

"Once again, Thomas Sawyer," the schoolmaster said, pointing to the girls' section, "you have outsmarted yourself."

Tom trudged down the aisle and slumped into the seat next to Becky. His plan had worked.

As soon as the schoolmaster began the lesson, Tom smiled at her.

Becky ignored him.

Taking the apple out of his pocket, Tom shined it on his sleeve and carefully placed it in front of her.

She returned it.

He put it back on her desk. Smiling sweetly, Becky picked it up and slipped it onto the desk of a plain girl in the next row. When the girl turned around to see who had given it to her, Becky pointed to Tom.

The plain girl stared goggle-eyed at Tom. Tom gazed at Becky with more admiration than ever.

◆ ◆ ◆

At the end of the school day, Becky was still ignoring him. But Tom hadn't given up yet. When school was dismissed, he ran ahead of her and waited on the footbridge over Murrell's Creek.

As Becky stepped onto the bridge, Tom lifted a leg and balanced himself on one foot. He imitated a tightrope walker doing a difficult and dangerous feat.

Becky pretended not to see. But as she walked past him, she reached out and gave him a quick shove. Tom teetered for a moment, then toppled into the creek.

Becky had done it again, and she smiled to herself as she heard Tom hit the water.

◆ ◆ ◆

Wet, but unhurt—except for his pride—Tom struggled to his feet, then stopped in surprise. Huck stood under the bridge, smoking a pipe.

"Hello, Huck!"

"Hello yourself and see how you like it," Huck replied.

Tom waded toward him. "What are you doing here?"

"Lookin' for fools."

"Under a bridge?"

Huck pointed to Tom. "I found one, didn't I?" He pulled the pipe out of his mouth. "You gonna let her get away with that?"

"It's 'cause she likes me," Tom explained.

"She pushed you off a bridge 'cause she likes you?" Huck asked incredulously.

Tom nodded.

"And you don't mind?"

"Not really, nope," Tom said.

"Then you're both crazy," Huck said finally.

Tom gestured at a burlap sack lying on the ground. "What's in the sack?"

"Dead cat."

Tom opened the sack—and closed it quickly. The smell alone was enough to kill a person.

"Wagon run him over," Huck told him. "Guts came out at both ends."

"What's a dead cat good for?"

"To cure warts with."

"I got a wart," Tom said. "How's it work?"

"You take your dead cat to the graveyard at midnight on the day somebody wicked's been buried," Huck explained solemnly. "And when the devil comes, you heave your dead cat at him and say, 'Devil, follow corpse, cat follow devil, warts follow cat. I'm done with ye!' That'll fetch any wart," Huck explained.

"Sounds right," Tom agreed. "When're you gonna try it?"

Huck tapped out his pipe. "Tonight."

"They buried old Hoss Williams today," Tom said slowly. "The devil's gonna want him for sure. Lemme go with you, Huck?"

"You might get scared."

Tom scowled at him. No one was going to leave him out of an adventure. "Not me! I ain't scared of nothin'!"

five

A Graveyard, a Murder, and Turtle Guts

Lightning flashed over the grounds of the Hannibal graveyard, as Tom and Huck climbed over a stone wall. Suddenly Tom let out a low terrified cry. Something had clutched him from behind.

Huck turned back. With one quick motion, he freed Tom from a tangle of vines.

"The dead seems kinda lively tonight," Huck confided. "But don't worry. I got just the thing. I learnt it from a witch woman." He closed his eyes and chanted. "Ghosts and goblins, stay away. In your graves I bid you stay. Haunt again some other day."

He opened his eyes. "That oughta do it."

The boys sighed with relief.

A moment later, footsteps sounded in the cemetery.

"Are you sure you got the words right?" Tom asked.

A dim otherworldly light flickered in the distance. Tom and Huck glanced fearfully at each other, then dove behind a mausoleum. Three shrouded figures emerged from the fog.

"What do we do now?" Tom asked, trying to keep the quaver out of his voice.

"Know any prayers?" Huck asked.

Tom dropped to his knees, closed his eyes, and began to rattle off a prayer.

Huck poked him. "Look."

The two boys peered over the top of the tomb.

"That ain't Hoss Williams they're diggin' up," Tom whispered. "They're goin' for one of them old graves."

A sudden flash of lightning illuminated the three figures at the grave.

"This is worse than ghosts," Tom muttered.

"Who are they?"

"The first two ain't so bad. Doc Robinson and Muff Potter. Muff wouldn't hurt a fly. But that third feller . . ." he paused. "That's Injun Joe."

Huck shuddered. "Injun Joe?"

"You know him?"

"Let's just say I met him once and I ain't anxious to meet him again."

◆ ◆ ◆

Muff and Injun Joe shoveled out the grave, while Doc Robinson stood over them with the lantern. A loud *thonk* rang out as Injun Joe's shovel hit wood.

Muff looked as if he wished he had never come. "Would it be all right if we took a break for a little libation?" he asked timidly. "I need me a drink."

"No," snapped Doc Robinson. "Haul it out. Hurry."

The two men lifted a rotted wooden coffin out of the grave and set it on the ground.

"Pry it open and tip it over," the undertaker ordered.

With his shovel, Injun Joe forced the lid open. Then he tipped the coffin over and dumped the skeleton on the ground. The bones fell with a clatter.

A small wooden box tumbled out after the bones. On its lid was engraved one word: *Murrell.*

"Murrell! One-Eye Murrell! By God!" Muff cried.

At the mausoleum, Tom turned excitedly to Huck. "One-Eye Murrell was a pirate. Him and his gang used to plunder up and down the river 'til the army came and killed 'em in an ambush. The treasure was never found."

Doc Robinson seized the box and shoved it under his coat. "Put the coffin back and cover your tracks."

He started to leave, but Injun Joe stepped in front of him. "Not so fast," he growled.

"Get out of my way," the undertaker said coldly.

"Give me the box." Injun Joe grabbed it with fingers of steel, but Doc Robinson wouldn't let go. The two men began to struggle fiercely.

"Doc—Joe—let's discuss this like gentlemen," Muff pleaded.

With one vicious blow, Injun Joe sent the undertaker toppling onto the ground.

"Now, Joe, what'd you do that for?" Muff said plaintively.

Injun Joe ignored him. He ripped open the box and pulled out a tattered, yellowed piece of paper. His cruel face lit with a sudden smile. "It's a map to the treasure," he said.

"Murrell's treasure! By glory, we're rich!" Muff cried.

At these words, Doc Robinson seized a wooden grave marker from a grave and staggered to his feet. "It's mine!" he shrieked, swinging the grave marker at Injun Joe.

Injun Joe ducked. The board connected solidly with Muff's head, and he tumbled unconscious to the ground.

Injun Joe leaped at Doc Robinson. The undertaker was no match for him. Injun Joe hit him until Doc Robinson slumped to the ground near the mausoleum where Tom and Huck hid.

Injun Joe pulled his knife out of his belt. Suddenly, he replaced it. With a small smile on his face, he walked over to where Muff lay unconscious and pulled out Muff's knife instead.

Then he went back to Doc Robinson and raised the knife over his head.

Behind the mausoleum, Tom and Huck saw the knife rise and fall three times over Doc Robinson. In mortal terror, the boys turned and ran. But to Tom's horror, his jacket caught on a branch and ripped.

Injun Joe lifted his head. He had heard a noise. He scrambled over the tomb just in time to see two figures vanish into the fog.

As he looked around, searching for a clue to their identity, his eye caught a glint of light on the ground. It was a black cat's-eye marble. Injun Joe picked it up and studied it intently.

On the ground, Muff groaned. Injun Joe tossed the bloody knife to Muff's side and ran off through the cemetery.

◆ ◆ ◆

In the woods, Huck and Tom ran as fast as they had ever run. Their hearts pounded, and their lungs felt ready to burst. But terror kept them moving. Every bush looked like a man ready to pounce on them; every branch was an arm reaching out.

Finally, they reached a familiar clearing. They ran through it, and into a small cave that had sheltered them before.

"We gotta tell the sheriff," Tom gasped, when he had caught his breath enough to speak.

"I ain't tellin' nobody nothin'," Huck answered roughly. "And unless you're dumber than I think, you'll keep your mouth shut, too."

"But we seen a murder!" Tom protested.

"Yeah—and there'll be two more if we was to squeak 'bout this. Believe me, Injun Joe wouldn't make any more of drownding us than a couple of cats!"

Tom stared at him. "Well, I guess you're right," he said finally. "I guess we shouldn't tell nobody."

"You better believe it," Huck said. "And just so you don't change your mind, we're gonna swear an oath. We'll write it down and sign it in blood."

"Our blood?" Tom quavered.

"Unless you want to go back and borrow some from Doc Robinson," Huck said grimly.

Huck picked up a pine shingle and held it out to Tom. "You do it. I ain't much good at writin'."

Tom felt his jacket pockets for a quill. "I lost my cat's-eye!" he suddenly exclaimed.

"We got bigger things to worry 'bout," Huck scolded him. "Now write this."

Tom picked up a sharp stick and began to write on the shingle. "Huck Finn and Tom Sawyer swear that they will keep shut about what they seen," dictated Huck, "and may they drop down dead if they ever tell."

"And rot," Tom added.

"And rot." Huck inspected the shingle. "You write good. Now, we sign it." Huck pulled out his knife. Carefully, he cut his finger, then passed the knife to Tom. With his bleeding finger, Tom wrote his initials on the shingle.

Huck stared at his finger, then at the shingle. For a moment, neither boy said anything. Then Tom grabbed Huck's finger and traced his initials on the shingle. "H is for Huck, F for Finn."

Huck was pleased and impressed. "Now we get to swear our loyalty to each other," Huck said.

Tom made up an oath: "Turtle guts. Frog slime. Chickens and hens. You and me will always be friends."

six

Professions of Love

Tom lay in his bed, unable to sleep. Outside, the wind howled and rain slashed against the window. Suddenly, Tom jerked upright, his breath coming in rapid gasps. Was that a man in the old tree outside the window? It was! Injun Joe stared straight at Tom.

Injun Joe leaped through the window, which shattered into a thousand pieces. The expression on Injun Joe's face was pure evil, pure hate. "I'm gonna kill you, Tom Sawyer!" he shrieked, raising his knife high.

Tom screamed as Injun Joe came toward him. The knife plunged down, down, down . . .

◆ ◆ ◆

Tom awoke screaming. A grinning Sid was sitting on the end of his bed. "Bad dream?" he inquired happily.

Still trembling from the dream, Tom snatched a pillow and swung it at his cousin.

◆ ◆ ◆

A little later, three children on their way to school stopped abruptly as Injun Joe stepped in front of them. In one hand he held a black cat's-eye marble. "This belong to any of you?" he asked in a low, chilling voice.

The children shook their heads and ran off as fast as they could.

As Tom walked to school, his mind was on his troubles: the murder he had seen, and the oath he had sworn never to speak of it. It just wasn't right . . .

"Hello, Tom," said a feminine voice.

It was Becky Thatcher, balancing on the rail of the bridge over Murrell's Creek.

"Becky." His eyes lit up.

"I'm sorry I pushed you in the creek yesterday," she said. "You can push me in if you want."

Tom shrugged. "I would—but I just don't feel

like it right now." He extended a hand to help her off the rail.

"Thank you." She studied his face for a moment. "What's wrong, Tom?"

". . . Nothin'."

Becky moved closer and took his hand sympathetically. "You can tell me. I won't ever tell anybody."

Tom sighed. He wished he could tell her—or her father, the judge—but he had sworn not to.

Becky fished in her lunch basket. "Here. This is for you." She handed a shiny red apple to him. He broke into a grin.

"You ever been engaged, Becky?"

"No." Her eyes sparkled. "How do you do it?"

"Well, you gotta tell the other person that you love them."

"And then what?" Becky asked.

"Well, then you're s'posed to kiss."

"Really?"

"Sure . . ."

"You first," she said shyly.

Tom took a deep breath. "I love you. There! Now you got to say it to me."

"Turn your face away," Becky commanded. Tom turned away. "But you can't tell anybody ever."

"I won't," Tom said.

Becky leaned close. "I love you," she whispered.

Tom beamed. "Well, I guess it's all done but the kissin' part."

The two gazed at each other. Slowly, Tom leaned forward. Becky moved close. Their lips touched. Then they quickly pulled away, a little scared by what they had done.

Tom thrust his hand into his pocket, pulled out a rusty doorknob, and held it out to Becky.

"Oh, Tom, it's . . . it's . . . what is it?" she cried.

"Your engagement ring."

"Oh, it's beautiful," Becky breathed.

"It sure is. Why, when I was engaged to Amy Lawrence . . ."

Becky's eyes widened and she stepped back. "You mean I'm not the first?"

"But, Becky," Tom protested. "That was ages ago. Two months at least."

Becky was on the verge of tears. She yelled at Tom, "I hate you! I hate you! I hope you die!" She flung the doorknob at his feet and ran off.

Tom just shook his head and mumbled to himself, "What'd I do?"

seven

That's What Friends Are For

Tom walked down Main Street, feeling even more glum than before. The murder. The oath. And now Becky. What next?

"Hey, Tom!" Joe Harper was waving wildly to him. "Come on! School's been called off!"

"Called off? What for?"

"There's been a murder!"

A cold chill ran up Tom's spine. He began to run with the other townspeople toward the graveyard.

The graveyard was swarming with excitement. Doc Robinson's body was covered with a sheet and lying near the dug-up grave.

"I didn't do it! I swear I didn't do it!" Muff's anguished voice cried.

"Sheriff, I caught Muff washing himself at my trough early this morning," a farmer declared.

The crowd gasped at this revelation. Schoolmaster Dobbins stepped forward. "Well, that sounds mighty suspicious, especially the washing, which is not a habit of Muff Potter's."

"No, wait a minute," Muff protested, but no one was listening to him.

Another man came forward. "Look here what I found! It's Muff Potter's knife! I sold it to him last winter."

"I say lynch him!" cried the schoolmaster. "Lynch him now!"

"You gotta believe me . . ." Muff pleaded.

Amid the cries to lynch Muff, Injun Joe stepped forward. "I saw the murder," he announced.

The crowd quieted, and made room for him to speak.

"Oh, Joe, thank the lord," said Muff in relief. "You tell 'em now, Joe, tell 'em."

"Tell us what you know," the sheriff echoed sternly.

Injun Joe began to speak. "I was passing by here last night and I saw Muff and Doc Robinson digging up that there grave. And then, in a drunken rage, I seen Muff Potter stab the doc."

Tom wanted to step forward and tell everyone the truth. But what about his oath? And what would Joe do?

"That ain't how it happened!" Muff cried. "I swear! We found the map to Murrell's treasure! And Joe and Doc got to fighting—"

"Murrell's treasure!" Injun Joe sneered. "Do you hear that, everybody? More drunk talk from Muff Potter!"

The schoolmaster piped up. "Murrell's treasure is an old wives' tale. I know the history of this entire county and I tell you it doesn't exist."

"I seen the map!" Muff said.

"You're lyin'," Injun Joe said flatly. "There ain't no treasure map. There never was." He glanced over at the tavern keeper, Emmett.

Emmett yelled out, "Everybody who thinks that Muff Potter is a drunk, a liar, and a murderer, raise yer hands!"

"Aye! Tar him! Lynch him! String him up!" The

crowd surged forward with a roar. Someone threw a rope around Muff's neck.

Muff looked around desperately. Who would save him now?

A gunshot rang out. The crowd quieted. Judge Thatcher lowered a smoking gun. He nodded to the crowd.

"Now, now, people. You wouldn't deny me the pleasure of presiding over his trial, would you? What good's having a judge if you don't let him judge?" Calmly, he pulled the rope from Muff's neck.

"We all know he's guilty!" shrieked Schoolmaster Dobbins.

A cane came down hard on his head, yanking off the schoolmaster's wig. "And we all know you're an idiot, Ed Dobbins!" announced the Widow Douglas, the richest and most-feared person in Hannibal.

Her white hair was pinned neatly back. Her black dress was simple and sober. Her words rang out stinging and strong. "Listen to me, you pointy-headed fools. Muff Potter may be the scum of the earth, but he still deserves a fair trial and I aim to see that he gets one." She turned to Judge Thatcher. "How soon can you get this show on the road?"

"I could start hearing evidence day after tomorrow."

"Settled!" With a withering glance, she turned on the crowd. "Now the rest of you 'good citizens' go about your business and let the law do its job!"

Slowly the crowd dispersed. The sheriff led Muff away. As he passed Tom, Muff cried out, "I didn't do it, Tom!"

His conscience in torment, Tom watched the sheriff haul Muff away. Suddenly, he couldn't stand it any longer and began to run after them.

But as he passed a tall grave marker, a leg kicked out and tripped him.

"You want to drop dead and rot?" It was Huck, holding up the pine-shingle oath.

"Muff's innocent. We got to do somethin' to help him!"

"We don't got to do nothin'," Huck said flatly.

"You'd let him hang for somethin' he didn't do?" Tom cried.

"Ain't no skin off me." Huck sat down on a gravestone.

"What if there was another way? A way that wouldn't make us break our oath?"

"What way is that?"

"What if we could get that treasure map?"

"Yeah!" Huck said sarcastically. "It would prove that Muff Potter was telling the truth and Injun Joe was lyin' and Muff'd be set free and Injun Joe would hang and we'd be heroes and the whole town'd be saved. That's a good idea, Tom."

"Thanks."

"Only one tiny little problem." Huck got to his feet. "The map is in Injun Joe's pocket."

"Well, if you're scared . . ." Tom called after Huck's retreating back.

Huck turned around and glared at Tom. "Why should I stick my neck out for Muff Potter?"

"'Cause we know Muff didn't do it!"

"So?"

"So, not doin' anything about it is wrong. We gotta help him," Tom insisted.

"Says who?" Huck demanded.

Tom sighed. Getting through to Huck wasn't easy. "What if it was *you* in Muff's shoes?"

"Well, it ain't," Huck said with exasperating logic.

"What if it was me?"

Huck looked uncomfortable. "If you was that stupid, you'd deserve what was comin' to you."

"That's not what friends do. I thought we were friends, Huck." Tom turned and walked away.

Huck frowned as he watched Tom go. "Maybe I don't know what you're talkin' about," he said softly.

eight

Follow That Map!

In the jailhouse, a scared, defeated Muff Potter sat huddled in his cell. The door clanged open. Muff looked up hopefully—but it was only the sheriff coming to deliver a meal of a biscuit and a cup of water.

"Has anybody come to see me, sheriff?" Muff asked.

"Don't be stupid, Muff." The door slammed shut. "Nobody cares about you. And nobody's gonna miss you when you're gone."

◆ ◆ ◆

Huck sat on the jailhouse roof, his tattered shirt blowing in the breeze. He had overheard every word. For a moment, he sat silently. Then he jumped lightly to his feet and ran off across the roof.

◆ ◆ ◆

In the street below, Injun Joe stepped purposefully in front of two strolling people and lit a cigar. The couple quickly crossed the street to avoid him.

"Evenin'!" Injun Joe called to them, enjoying their fear. He exhaled a cloud of foul black smoke and laughed cruelly.

As he made his way down the street, a silent figure in tattered clothing followed him from the rooftops.

◆ ◆ ◆

Tom sat under the Murrell's Creek bridge, throwing pebbles in the water, when a head appeared, upside down, over the edge of the bridge.

"Injun Joe's on the move," Huck told him urgently. His head disappeared.

Tom leaped up to follow him.

◆ ◆ ◆

"What made you change your mind?" Tom asked him as the two boys sneaked through the woods behind the tavern in pursuit of Injun Joe.

Huck shrugged. "I figgered if you did it

alone you'd probably just botch it up."

Tom hid a smile. "Yeah, probably."

They slipped into an alleyway behind the tavern. The two boys found a wooden box, shoved it under a window, then climbed up to peer into the tavern.

The tavern was crowded. Trappers, traders, and rivermen were eating, drinking, and playing cards. And Injun Joe and Emmett were sitting at a table right below the window.

Emmett drank from a pitcher of beer and studied the treasure map. Then he slid it over to Injun Joe. He spoke a few words. Injun Joe nodded, and then, deep in thought, rolled the black cat's-eye marble absently between his fingers.

"He's got my cat's-eye!" Tom whispered in horror. He tottered and lost his balance. Vainly, he grabbed at the gutter to steady himself, but it broke off in his hand. He and Huck went sprawling.

Like a bad dream, the gutter knocked a piece of wood through the window, spraying Injun Joe and Emmett with broken glass.

The two men leaped up to investigate.

"Probably a drunk," Emmett said as they stepped through the tavern door.

"Well, it wasn't Muff Potter," Injun Joe said with a dark smile.

"No. The only stumblin' he'll be doin' is at the end of a rope." Emmett laughed hard at his joke.

Injun Joe turned on him. "Shaddup," he growled.

Emmett's mouth snapped shut.

"Well, I gotta be goin'. I'll see ya tomorrow—partner." There was an undercurrent of menace in Injun Joe's voice.

"Right, Injun Joe," Emmett said uneasily. "Tomorrow."

As Injun Joe vanished into the woods, Emmett took a swig from his beer and winced. A piece of broken glass had fallen into it. He poured the beer into a rain barrel and went back into the tavern.

Their hair plastered to their heads and reeking of beer, Huck and Tom climbed out of the barrel and took off after Joe.

◆ ◆ ◆

As the sun set, Injun Joe slid into a dugout and pushed off from a crowded dock. Hidden nearby, Huck and Tom watched him as he glided past.

"I guess we could take Muff's boat," whispered Tom.

"Yeah, he won't be using it any time soon," Huck whispered back.

Tom manned the rudder, while Huck leaned forward, keeping Injun Joe's dugout in sight. It was dark when Injun Joe landed on a wooded island. The two boys followed him ashore by moonlight.

"Stumblin' on Injun Joe in the dark ain't my idea of a good time," Huck said. "We'll find us a place to camp and wait 'til first light."

As they tramped inland, the boat, with Tom's hat on the seat, came unmoored and floated away.

◆ ◆ ◆

Morning light streamed through the trees. Tom yawned and stretched. "Huck?" he said, looking around.

Huck was nowhere to be seen. "Huck!" Tom called, a note of panic entering his voice.

Suddenly, Huck dropped out of a tree right in front of Tom. He was covered from head to toe in mud and leaves. Except for the whites of his eyes, he looked like part of the forest.

Tom stared, speechless, then broke into a wide grin. Huck raised his dripping hand and wiped it across Tom's face.

◆ ◆ ◆

Camouflaged with mud and leaves, the two boys crept close to where Injun Joe snored beside his still, an empty bottle at his side.

"He's drunk asleep," Huck whispered. "Shouldn't be too hard to get that map."

"Yeah," Tom agreed. "Let's get it and git."

He took a step forward, then turned back. "Aren't you coming?" he said to his friend.

Huck looked at Injun Joe. "One map don't need the two of us. I'll wait here."

With a grimace at Huck, Tom started moving forward. A twig snapped underfoot. He froze.

Injun Joe sat up and stared bleary-eyed right through Tom. Then he fell back on the ground into a stupor.

Tom crept forward once more. A corner of the map was sticking out of Joe's pocket. It would be easy to pull it out. He almost had it. As Tom extended his hand, a drop of mud dripped down from his arm and onto Injun Joe's face.

Once more, Tom froze. If Joe woke up this time, nothing could save him. But Joe licked the mud off his lips and went on snoring.

Tom reached for the map. His fingers closed over the paper. Slowly and carefully, he drew it out of Joe's pocket. Suddenly there was an irresistible tickle in his nose. "AAAAAA-CHOOOO!"

He leaped back, banging into the still, which crashed to the ground. Whiskey spurted out; pots and ladles clashed and clanked.

With lightning speed, Huck jumped out and yanked Tom into the foliage. Both boys froze, afraid to even breathe.

"Wild boars!" Injun Joe swore, stumbling to his feet. In a rage, he threw his knife at a distant tree. The knife spun over and over, and then slammed directly into the center of a painted bull's-eye.

The boys' eyes bulged with fear.

Injun Joe picked up his rifle and pulled the knife out of the tree. Then he stalked off.

◆ ◆ ◆

"Where did he go?" Tom asked. He was embarrassed and ashamed that he had ruined their plans by sneezing. And Huck had hardly spoken to him all the way back to the shore.

Huck pointed toward the water. Injun Joe was in his dugout, paddling away from the island.

"Here." Huck held up his sleeve.

"What's that for?"

"So's you can wipe your nose."

Tom smiled. He had been forgiven. The two boys tramped down to the water.

◆ ◆ ◆

Tom and Huck paddled logs toward the bank where Injun Joe's dugout lay.

"I think I'll live like you for a while," Tom said. "You really got it made."

"Huh?" Huck said.

"Doin' what you please. Nobody to tell you when to go to bed," Tom recited. "Nobody to make you go to school or change your shirt or clean your ears or eat your dinner."

"Yep," Huck agreed. "This here's the way to live. Nobody's gonna tell me what to do or where to go, or when to be there." As if trying to convince himself, he added, "You'll never catch me cooped up in some stuffy old house with some liver-lipped old lady makin' me eat whatever's on the plate in front of me."

"You don't know how lucky you are," Tom told him, never noticing that Huck didn't seem quite so sure of that.

Huck turned away. After a moment, he said gruffly, "That's right."

Tom pointed to the shore. "Looks like he's headin' for the hills."

The boys slipped off their logs and waded ashore. They rushed past the dugout and followed Injun Joe into the forest.

nine

X Marks the Spot

"I don't see his prints." Huck sighed in frustration. A heavy rain was falling and it was night. He and Tom had been tracking Injun Joe for what seemed like days. "He must've turned off on that road a mile back."

Tom pointed to an old, decrepit mansion overgrown with vines and creepers. "That's the old Hawkshaw place. It's supposed to be haunted."

Huck snorted. "That ain't no big deal. Ghosts don't come out 'til night."

Something rattled and clanked on the path behind them.

"What's that?" Tom hissed.

"I dunno." Even Huck was scared. "But it's getting closer."

"Then what are we standin' here for?" The two boys ran for the haunted house in the pouring rain. As they entered it, shutters slammed open and shut as if to warn them.

Dusty cobwebs were woven across cracked walls. Rats scurried from room to room. Weeds had sprung up from the floorboards.

"See? It ain't so bad," Huck said bravely. "Not a ghost in sight."

As if in response to his words, the front door fell off its hinges and crashed to the floor. Tom and Huck jumped in terror and then bolted up a rickety staircase.

They ran down a hallway and pushed open a door. A ghost billowed out at them.

"Yaaaaahhhh!" they screamed. Then they exchanged sheepish glances. It was only a ripped sheet blowing out from a canopy bed.

"Listen!" Huck whispered. They dropped to their knees and looked down through a hole in the floor.

Injun Joe and Emmett entered the house carrying shovels and picks.

Tom struggled to flee, but Huck held him tight.

"What was that?" Injun Joe asked. He looked up, toward the boys. They shrank back into the darkness.

"They say this place is haunted," Emmett said uneasily.

"By rats, maybe," Injun Joe scoffed. "Let's get to work." He pulled out the treasure map and unfolded it. "Accordin' to Murrell's map, it should be right next to the fireplace."

Emmett hefted his pick and brought it down forcefully on the floor near the fireplace. Injun Joe laid the map on a table and went over to help him.

Upstairs, Tom and Huck exchanged excited looks. The map was almost directly below them. Huck dug in his pocket and brought out a fishing line with a hook. As the two men dug up the floor, the line with its hook slowly descended from above.

"You sure about the fireplace?" Emmett whined.

"Ain't that what I said?" Injun Joe snarled.

"Well, if this is the right place, he sure buried it deep. I'm halfway to China."

Injun Joe shot him a fierce look. "Keep diggin'." He went over to the table to check the map. A small fishing hook snagged his hat.

Above him, Huck and Tom exchanged worried looks. What should they do now?

"See? Right here!" Injun Joe snatched up the map and waved it at Emmett. "Fireplace!"

"Think I hit something!" Emmett cried as his pick clanged down on something metal. As he turned to Joe, his face blanched.

Emmett whimpered and pointed above Joe. Injun Joe's hat was floating a foot above his head.

Injun Joe looked up. His hat dropped onto his face. With a snarl, he tore it off and threw it to the floor.

Emmett screamed.

His partner stomped over to him and hit him hard in the face. Then Injun Joe stared up through the hole in the ceiling to the room above.

Shaking with fear, Tom and Huck retreated into the darkness. But Joe only swiped at a few cobwebs hanging from the ceiling and then picked up his hat. "You screaming coward," he said contemptuously to Emmett. "Look, it wasn't ghosts—it was cobwebs. Now come on."

The two men continued digging. In a few moments, they had freed a heavy metal box. Setting it on the floor, Emmett smashed the lock with his pick and Joe opened the lid.

The chest was filled with gold and silver coins. It was a fortune—even a few of the coins would have been a fortune. In the room above, Tom and Huck caught their breath.

"Murrell's treasure," Tom whispered.

"Look at you, you beautiful money," Injun Joe said.

"Hello, Texas and the good life!" Emmett cried.

Grabbing a handful of coins, Injun Joe stuffed them in his pocket and then slammed the lid shut. "We'll wait 'til after the trial. I got to testify. Make sure Muff takes the blame for Doc's murder."

"Where we gonna keep it in the meantime?" Emmett asked.

"At Number Two under the cross. Load it on the wagon. I got some things to take care of in town."

As Emmett staggered toward the door with the heavy chest, Injun Joe picked up his lantern,

With a whistle and a smile, Tom tries to convince his friend Billy that there is nothing more fun than whitewashin' a fence.

Tom, smug and relaxed, languishes under a tree while his friends enjoy the whitewashin'.

Tom and his friends Ben and Joe stare in awe as they see a black carriage start down the street. Inside is the beautiful Becky Thatcher, quietly eating an apple.

Ben and Joe tease Tom, forcing him to play middleman for a while before they trade Becky's fallen apple.

Huck sits back in his "throne" and tells Tom about his life as a free man.

Tom strolls into school late, with an apple in his pocket and a mischievous plan up his sleeve.

Pretending not to notice Becky as she starts across the bridge, Tom shows off for her.

Tom and Becky shyly confess their feelings for each other.

At first perplexed, Becky accepts her doorknob engagement "ring" from Tom.

Outside the back of the tavern, Emmett and Injun Joe scheme to steal Murrell's treasure.

A camouflage of mud and leaves saves Tom and Huck from the fatally precise throw of Injun Joe's knife.

Tom returns from the dead—right through the ceiling of the church!

Determined to seek justice, Tom leaps to his feet and points to the murderer.

Tom and Becky cautiously wind their way through the dark tunnels of MacDougal's cave.

Out of danger at last, Becky runs into Tom's arms and gives him a big kiss on the cheek.

then reached into a pocket and pulled out the treasure map. Carefully, he put one corner of the map into the flame. As the flame caught and spread, Injun Joe tossed the map over his shoulder and went out the door.

The last piece of evidence that could have saved Muff was gone, turned to ashes.

Tom's shoulders slumped. "No more map."

"No more treasure," Huck said sadly.

"No more Muff."

The two boys trudged dejectedly back to town.

"Number Two, under the cross?" Tom asked his friend.

"If you ask me," Huck said soberly, "we're better off not knowin'."

"Why?"

"'Cause we're pushin' our luck. We done all we could," Huck said. "Messin' with Injun Joe is the best way I know to end up dead."

"Yeah," Tom agreed. "They say he's the best knife-fighter on the Mississippi."

"No." Huck's face was somber. "My pap's the best. He taught Injun Joe everythin' he knows."

"Your pap knew Injun Joe?"

Huck looked down at the ground. "Him and

Injun Joe met in jail. Pap was always runnin' from the law—'cept when he was beating me like a rented mule. He taught Joe how to throw a knife . . ." With lightning speed Huck drew his knife and threw it at the mile marker twenty feet away.

Tom watched in amazement as the knife spun end over end, and finally quivered in the dead center of the marker.

He ran to the marker, yanked out the knife, and held it out to Huck.

"He taught me, too," Huck said simply.

The boys walked on. Tom gazed at Huck with new respect.

As they approached Hannibal, bells began to toll.

"You hear that?" Tom said.

"Church bells."

Tom frowned. "But it ain't Sunday."

"Them's funeral bells," Huck said.

"You're right." The two boys looked at each other. Who was dead now? They began to run in the direction of town.

ten

Back from the Dead

Tom Sawyer hid in the church attic with Huck and watched the mourners come into the church. Organ music blared as Aunt Polly, Sid, and Tom's cousin Mary made their way to the front of the church, sobbing loudly.

"It's me!" Tom said in astonishment. "They think I'm dead!" He rubbed his hands together in glee. "Can you believe it? Boy, this is the best trick that's ever been pulled in the history of Hannibal. They really miss me! What do you think of that?"

"I dunno." Huck shrugged. "I ain't never been missed."

The sound of excited voices came from outside. Tom peered through a crack in the wall. Several kids were standing outside the church.

"Tom Sawyer beat me up once! He knocked out two of my front teeth."

"That's nothin'," said another kid. "He knocked out all my teeth and broke my arms."

"If I'd known he'd be braggin' about it," Tom whispered to Huck, "I'd really have done it."

Suddenly he stopped speaking. A saddened and tearful Becky had joined the group of children below. "I wish I could see him just one more time," she sobbed. "I'd call him my sweetheart and kiss him, right in front of everybody."

Tom beamed. Being dead was the best thing that had ever happened to him.

◆ ◆ ◆

In the churchyard, another kind of conversation was taking place. Injun Joe held Tom's black cat's-eye marble aloft between two fingers, while with his other hand he slapped coins into Joe Harper's palm.

"Mickey Douglas got the cat's-eye from his cousin in St. Louis," Joe recited, staring at the money. "Then he traded it to Alfred Temple who sold it to Doug Tanner who traded it to Johnny Miller who—no, wait. Alfred sold it to Johnny who traded it to Doug . . ."

Injun Joe seized him by the collar. "Just tell me who owned it last," he snarled.

"Tom Sawyer," Joe blurted. "Tom Sawyer owned it last."

Injun Joe's eyes widened in surprise.

Joe Harper watched the mourners file into church. "But it don't matter 'cause now Tom's dead."

Injun Joe's face broke into an evil grin. "Too bad. I'm so sad." He snatched the coins from Joe's hand and shoved him away.

◆ ◆ ◆

Judge Thatcher stood at the pulpit. "Tom Sawyer wasn't a bad boy." He glanced at his daughter Becky. "Not from what I'm told. He was just mischievous and willful. In that respect, I guess you'd have to admit there's a little bit of Tom Sawyer in all boys." He paused. "I know I speak for everybody when I say we're going to miss him."

Above in the attic, Tom grinned. "I'm beginnin' to miss me, too."

Huck looked at him in annoyance. "How

long are you gonna make your aunt suffer?"

Tom looked down. Aunt Polly was sobbing in the pew. "She does look sad," he admitted. "Don't cry, Aunt Polly," he said in a low voice. "I'm okay."

"You got all these folks bawlin' their eyes out," Huck told him sternly. "Go home, Tom."

In the pulpit below, Judge Thatcher looked heavenward. "Lord, we'd do anything to have Tom back."

As the judge spoke, Huck reached out and shoved Tom. Tom fell over the plaster ceiling, which gave way beneath his weight. He tumbled down into the church, landing in front of the pulpit.

Aunt Polly let out a scream, and almost the entire congregation rushed over to hug and kiss Tom. In the uproar, Huck slipped away. No one missed him.

Becky pushed through the crowd. Tom pulled away from his aunt's embrace. "Hello, Becky. Ain't you glad to see me?"

In reply, she punched him in the nose. Tom staggered back, blood streaming from his face. Becky had got the better of him again. Then she stormed off with her father.

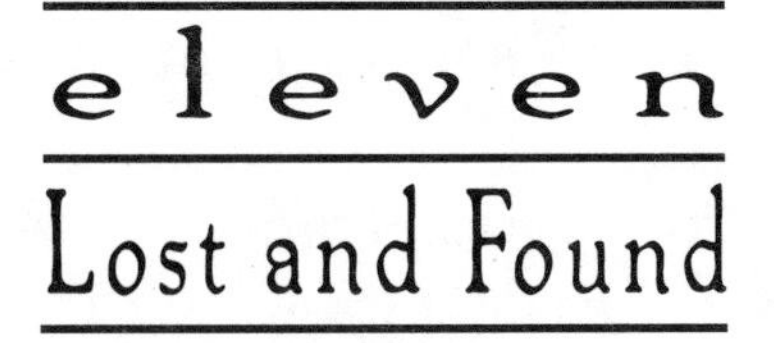

eleven
Lost and Found

Tom tramped through the forest. He was clean of every trace of dirt and mud. Last night, Aunt Polly had given him a bath he would never forget. Tugging to loosen his collar, he entered Huck's camp. Huck was shoving some belongings into a burlap sack.

"Huck. What're you doin'?"

Huck didn't look up. "Packin'."

"What for?"

"Time to move on down the river," he answered curtly.

Tom stared at his friend. "Why?"

"Why?" Huck repeated. "'Cause it's what I do. I

never stay long in one place. Gotta keep movin'."

"What about Muff Potter?"

"We tried," Huck said in a flat voice. "It didn't work out."

"But, Huck," Tom pleaded, "you can't go. What about the trial tomorrow? And there's a town picnic on Saturday . . ."

"I suppose I'm gonna sit with you while you introduce me to all them good townsfolk, huh?"

"But, Huck . . ."

"I don't leave places 'cause I want to," he said angrily. "I leave 'cause sooner or later they find me and run me out. This time I'm gonna beat 'em to the punch."

"I thought we was friends," Tom said.

Huck stared coldly at him. "You thought wrong—I ain't got no friends. Ain't got time for 'em."

He picked up his sack and turned to leave. Then he stopped. "But if I did have one, I'd want him to be like you."

With those parting words, Huck Finn disappeared into the forest.

◆ ◆ ◆

Tom was stunned. He had never thought that Huck would walk out on him like this. For a few minutes, he couldn't move at all. Then he turned to go. Injun Joe was waiting for him.

"Yaaaah!" Tom screamed.

Injun Joe picked him up and threw him to the ground.

A terrified Tom inched backward until Huck's throne was at his back.

Injun Joe reached into his pocket, pulled out the black cat's-eye marble, and tossed it at Tom. "You lose somethin'?"

Tom shook his head wildly. "That ain't mine."

Injun Joe pulled out his knife. "Don't lie to me, boy."

"You know, you're right," babbled Tom. "That is my cat's-eye. Reason I didn't recognize it right away is 'cause I lost it in the graveyard. Musta been two or three months ago."

Suddenly Injun Joe hurled his knife. Tom squeezed his eyes shut, then opened them as he heard a knife splintering wood. Joe had thrown the knife at a nearby tree. It had landed right near Tom's head.

"Fetch me the knife," Injun Joe commanded.

Tom couldn't move. His legs and arms felt like water.

"I said fetch it!" Joe hissed.

Tom shakily got to his feet. On trembling legs, he walked over to the tree and pulled the knife out. Then he brought it over to Injun Joe.

"You'd like to stick it in me, wouldn't you?" Injun Joe asked. "Like to gut me good. Here's your chance." He looked at Tom, daring him. "Go ahead. All you gotta do is kill me and then tell everybody in Hannibal what you know."

Tom was paralyzed with fear. With one quick motion, Joe snatched the knife from his hand and pressed the blade to Tom's throat.

Then he whispered hoarsely in his ear: "You didn't kill me, boy. Big mistake. 'Cause if you ever say what you know, I'm sure gonna kill you."

With a bloodcurdling scream, Injun Joe vanished into the woods as if he had never been there.

twelve
Under Oath

"Hey, Muff . . ." Tom Sawyer's face appeared in the barred window above Muff Potter's jail bed. "How're you doin', Muff?"

"Not so good," Muff Potter answered.

"They treatin' you okay?"

Muff cast a terrified glance upward. "It's an awful thing that's happened, and now I've got to swing for it. Tom, they're gonna hang me."

Tom couldn't speak. "Maybe not," he stammered finally.

"I'm innocent," Muff cried out. "I didn't do it, I swear. I done some drunk, crazy things in my time, but I never killed anyone. You gotta believe me."

"I do," Tom said.

"You do?"

Tom nodded.

"How come?"

"Well, I know you, Muff," he said slowly. "Sometimes when you're drunk you get kinda disgustin' and you smell, too, but I know you wouldn't hurt a fly."

Muff smiled sadly. "Well, let's not talk about this, Tom. I don't want to make you feel bad, when you've befriended me." Tears began to roll down his face.

"Don't cry, Muff," Tom said awkwardly. "Please don't cry."

Muff wiped away the tears with the back of his hand. "You've been mighty good to me, Tom—better'n anybody else in this town, and I won't forget it. Let me shake your hand, Tom. Yours'll come through the bars, but mine's too big." He caught Tom's hand and held it tight. "Little hands," he said. "But I know they'd help Muff Potter a power if they could."

◆ ◆ ◆

Later that evening, Tom lay in bed, staring out the window.

The door opened and Aunt Polly came in. She

looked worried. "Why Tom," she said, "it's not bedtime for another hour. Are you feeling all right?"

She sat on the edge of the bed and put her hand on his forehead. "You don't have a fever. What's ailing you?"

For a moment, Tom debated silently. Should he tell her? Or shouldn't he?

"Aunt Polly," he finally said, "what if you swore an oath, promisin' not to tell somethin'? But the somethin' you promised not to tell needs tellin'."

Aunt Polly thought for a moment. "I guess you can't break the oath?"

Tom shook his head. "You drop dead. And rot."

"Not good."

"Yeah, and on top of that, somebody'll cut your throat with a knife."

"Not good at all," she agreed.

"But if you don't tell," Tom continued desperately, "somethin' worse might happen—to someone who don't deserve it."

Aunt Polly stared down at her hands. Then she looked directly at Tom. "For as long as I can remember, Tom, you've been nothing but trouble to me. Most of the time, you're selfish and irresponsible." She paused and ruffled his hair. "But, deep down, you're a good boy. You've got a good heart. And I believe you'll know the right thing to do and you'll do it."

She got up and went to the door. "Just follow your heart."

As she closed the door gently behind her, Tom gulped, "Muff's a goner."

◆ ◆ ◆

The town hall was packed. All of Hannibal had come to see the trial. Muff Potter, looking as if he hadn't slept in several weeks, sat in chains next to his lawyer. Injun Joe was with the other witnesses.

The prosecutor, Mr. Sneed, held up Muff's knife. "And you are sure, beyond any shadow of a doubt, that this is the implement upon which a transaction, resulting in purchase, between yourself and the accused took place?" he asked pompously.

"I, uh, could you repeat the question, please?" the witness said.

Mr. Sneed sighed. "You're sure this is the knife you sold?"

"Sure, I'm sure. Last winter."

"And is the beneficiary of the aforementioned transaction present here today?"

"If you're askin' me 'bout Muff Potter, I can tell you . . ."

Mr. Sneed sighed again. "Could you point out the owner of this knife, please?"

"Are ya blind? He's sittin' right there!"

◆ ◆ ◆

A few minutes later, Injun Joe came up to the stand. "So I headed up to the cemetery. I like to sit up there and watch the stars."

From the doorway where he was watching the trial, Tom's eyes narrowed. What a liar.

"Anyways, I saw Muff drunk. Real drunk and in a rage. I saw him lift the knife and then he stuck it in the doc, over and over again, 'bout four times he stuck 'im."

Mr. Sneed turned to the defense. "Take the witness."

"No questions," the defense said.

Judge Thatcher frowned. The crowd muttered. Even though they wanted to see Muff hang, they wanted his lawyer to put up a good fight first.

The Widow Douglas stood up. "Mr. Aycock, I would be obliged if you would at least pretend to defend Mr. Potter!"

There were shouts and catcalls from the crowd. Judge Thatcher pounded his gavel. "Order! Order in the court!"

Injun Joe walked back to his chair. He was smiling.

Mr. Sneed stepped forward. "By oaths of citizens whose simple word is above suspicion, we have fastened this awful crime beyond all possibility of question upon the unhappy prisoner. Muff Potter is guilty of the murder of Doctor Jonas Robinson. We rest our case here!"

"Counsel for the defense," said the judge, "Do you have a defense?"

The defense slowly rose. "Indeed we do, your honor. The defense calls to the stand—Thomas Sawyer!"

The crowd gasped. Aunt Polly turned pale.

As he walked to the stand, Tom glanced at Injun Joe, who shot him a vicious look.

"Thomas Sawyer, do you swear to tell the truth, the whole truth, and nothing but the truth, so help you God?"

Tom's hand trembled on the Bible. "I . . . I . . ." He looked again at Injun Joe, who slowly drew out his knife.

"Tom, do you swear to tell the truth?" Judge Thatcher repeated.

"It would certainly be the first time," the schoolmaster whispered loudly.

The crowd laughed. Tom flashed an angry look at Mr. Dobbins, clenched his jaw and said, "I do!"

The defense stepped forward. "Mr. Sawyer, where were you on the twenty-eighth of this month at the hour of midnight?"

Tom mumbled a few words.

"Louder, please, Tom," said Judge Thatcher.

"I was . . . uh . . . in the graveyard."

Aunt Polly's eyes widened.

"And what were you doing there?"

"Tryin' to get rid of warts."

Loud laughter came from the crowd. Tom glowered at them, then glanced once more at Injun Joe, who drew out his knife a little further.

"Were you close to that grave that Muff Potter was digging up?"

Tom's eyes were locked on Joe's knife. "I . . . I . . ."

Schoolmaster Dobbins rose impatiently. "This is a waste of time. Thomas Sawyer wouldn't know the truth if it kicked him in the teeth! This boy is an outright liar!"

That did it. Tom jumped to his feet. "I was there!" he cried. "I saw the murder. And Doc Robinson wasn't stabbed four times, he was stabbed three times!"

The sheriff stood up. "He's right! And I ain't told that to a soul!"

"Injun Joe and the doc got into a fight," Tom continued. "It wasn't Muff. Muff even tried to stop it, but the doc knocked him out cold." Tom grabbed the Bible and pointed it at Injun Joe.

"Injun Joe took Muff's knife and killed the doc!" he cried. "It was Injun Joe!"

In a fury, Injun Joe leaped up and threw his knife with deadly aim. It whistled through the air toward Tom, who held up the Bible in front of his face. The knife slammed into the holy book and came out an inch from Tom's nose on the other side.

As the crowd screamed, Injun Joe charged across the packed courtroom. When he couldn't get out fast enough, he ran across the laps of the spectators, pausing only to smash the schoolmaster in the nose.

"My node! He broke my node!" Mr. Dobbins yelled.

Then Injun Joe broke through a large window

and landed outside in a shower of broken glass and wood. But instead of running off, he looked menacingly back at Tom.

For a moment, Tom heard the terrifying voice from his nightmare: “I’m gonna kill you, Tom Sawyer!” Then Injun Joe was gone.

thirteen
Huck Returns

On the Mississippi River, a flatboat loaded with sacks and barrels docked at a small pier. Some men jumped off and began unloading. A few rivermen were waiting to help them.

"Say!" one of the rivermen said. "You come down from Hannibal?"

"Passed through just yesterday," the flatboatman answered.

"They hang Muff Potter yet?"

"You ain't heard?" the flatboatman said. "Muff didn't do it. It was Injun Joe stabbed Doc Robinson. A young boy, name of Tom Sawyer, said he seen Injun Joe do the killin'."

Huck Finn, smoking a pipe on the docks, stopped in his tracks.

"I'll be . . ." said the riverman. "Say! When they gonna hang that Injun Joe? I'd pay to see that."

"Ain't gonna happen. He got away."

A chill ran up Huck's spine. Tom was in trouble. He had to go back.

◆ ◆ ◆

Aunt Polly, Sid, Mary, and Tom were getting ready for the town picnic in Aunt Polly's kitchen.

"Mary, you can help me with the flowers," Aunt Polly said. "You did a fine job last year. Sid, you and Tom take the jam, and Tom, mind you don't eat any on the way there."

"I ain't goin'," Tom announced flatly.

"Not going to the picnic?" Sid said in mock horror.

"Shut your head, Sid."

"Tom, I know you're scared, and rightly so," Aunt Polly said, "but you're a glittering hero right now and the whole town will be wanting to see you. It's not your place to be worrying about that Injun Joe. I hear a detective came up from St. Louis—they say he found a clue."

"You can't hang a clue for murder," Tom muttered.

◆ ◆ ◆

That night, Tom lay wide-awake staring into the darkness. Sid snored peacefully in the bed beside him, but Tom couldn't even close his eyes. It was as though he were waiting for something. A branch snapped in the tree outside. Tom leaped up. He looked at the tree and saw a silhouette of a man. Was it real? Or was he imagining it? Tom pinched himself hard. It wasn't a dream.

Another snap, and then a bump. Tom dove under the covers. The window creaked as someone slowly opened it . . .

Tom gathered his courage and looked out from under the blankets. A dark figure came through the window. He opened his mouth to scream.

"Shhhh," said a familiar voice, and then: "Scared?" it whispered angrily. "You should be."

Tom caught his breath. "Huck? What are you doing?"

Huck shoved the pine shingle with their oath in front of Tom. "Remember this?"

"Yeah, but Huck . . ."

"Accordin' to this, you should be dead and startin' to rot about now."

"I had to help Muff," Tom said quietly. "Not to help him would have been wrong."

". . . I know, I know," Huck admitted. "But you swore an oath. Don't that mean anything?"

"Yes, of course, Huck, but—it just seemed like the right thing to do."

Huck sat down on the end of Tom's bed and stared into the darkness.

Tom put his hand on his friend's shoulder. "Huck," he repeated softly. "It was the right thing to do."

His friend shook his head. "No, you swore an oath, Tom. You swore."

"How could I just lay back and let Muff Potter swing? You tell me, Huck."

Huck jumped to his feet and paced up and down the room. "You know you ain't never been in more trouble. Injun Joe'll hunt you down and kill you f'sure. That's what he does."

"You think I don't know that?"

"Well, don't expect me to stick around and save you."

"I don't," Tom said angrily.

"Good—'cause I ain't going to."

Tom stared at him. "Then why'd you come back?"

"I dunno," Huck shrugged. "I guess just to tell you to be careful. I been to your funeral once, I ain't goin' again."

With those words, Huck vaulted out the window and slid down the tree.

Tom ran to the window. "Huck!"

His friend stopped.

"Muff's my friend," Tom called. "When a friend is in trouble, you don't run away."

For a moment, Huck didn't move. Then he vanished into the darkness.

◆ ◆ ◆

It was the afternoon of the spring picnic. Tables were heaped with food; kids bobbed for apples and danced around the maypole; a marching band played music. A sober Muff Potter entertained a group of children; while Becky and a group of older girls scattered hemp seeds and looked into mirrors to find out who their future husbands would be. All the mirrors reflected empty fields, and the girls giggled and scattered.

Only Becky stayed behind, glancing once more into her mirror.

Suddenly Tom raced across the field, chasing

Sid. At the sight of Becky, he stopped and she caught him in her mirror.

"Oh, no!" she cried.

"What's wrong?" Tom asked playfully. "Am I that bad to look at?"

"We're going to be married!"

"What??"

"Well, you needn't look so disappointed," Becky huffed. "I don't like it any better than you do."

She ran off, leaving a baffled Tom behind.

"What's wrong with you?" Joe Harper said, coming up to Tom.

Tom shook his head. "I think I just got married and divorced at the same time."

Before Joe could ask him what he was talking about, Muff yelled, "Children! Who's ready for the cave?"

A cheering, thronging mass of children gathered around him and followed him up a trail toward a cave in the side of the mountain.

◆ ◆ ◆

At dusk, a few adults, carrying torches, watched the children playing in the caves. The children's laughter echoed through the chambers.

Judge Thatcher called out to his daughter. "Be careful, Rebecca."

"Remember, kids, stay to the forechambers!" added Muff.

Becky raced around a stone column. Tom was waiting for her. "Be careful, Rebecca," he mocked. "Stay to the forechambers with the other children, Rebecca."

Becky flashed him a defiant look. "I'll go where I please." She peered down a dark and scary-looking tunnel. "Come on!" she called to one of her girlfriends. "Let's go down that tunnel!"

The friend shook her head. "Not me."

"Maybe I'll go down it myself." Becky looked at Tom.

"I dare ya," he said.

She tossed her head, picked up a lantern, and ran off down the dark tunnel. Immediately, she wished she could turn back—but she didn't want Tom to see her fear.

Tom watched her admiringly for a moment. Becky really had spirit. But he couldn't let her go down there alone. He took off after her.

Neither Tom nor Becky heard Muff calling to the other children that it was time to go.

fourteen
The Cave

Emmett stood in front of the bar, loading a shovel and pick into a burlap sack. The tavern was empty; it was night. He had closed early because of the town picnic.

Just then, the door creaked open and a shadow fell over the bar.

"Get out!" Emmett said irritably. "Can't you see, we're clos—"

The man stepped into the light.

"Joe!" Emmett cried. He didn't sound happy to see his partner.

Injun Joe paced back and forth like a ferocious

caged animal. "Gonna do a little diggin' without me?" he asked.

"No, Joe. I was, I was . . ." Emmett stuttered. Beads of sweat popped out on his forehead. "I was just gettin' the tools ready for when you came back. Boy, am I glad to see you."

"I don't think you're glad to see me," Injun Joe said softly and menacingly. "I think you was gonna go to Number Two under the cross and get the treasure for yourself."

"Joe, I wouldn't cheat you," Emmett protested. Slowly, he backed up toward the bar. There was a gun hidden there.

"That's right," Injun Joe said. "You wouldn't cheat me. 'Cause you're smart enough to know that if you did—"

Emmett whirled to grab his gun. But before he could even touch it, Injun Joe's knife sailed through the air and plunged into his back.

Injun Joe walked over to the body and pulled his knife out. ". . . I'd have to kill you," he finished.

◆ ◆ ◆

"It's beautiful," Becky said. She and Tom had just stepped into an enormous cavern.

Tom shrugged. "I've been here plenty of times," he bragged. "It's called Satan's Cathedral."

Becky's lip curled. "Well, I'll find a cavern you haven't been to and I'll name it myself." She crossed the cavern and entered another tunnel.

◆ ◆ ◆

The townsfolk were enjoying their bonfire. Sparks leaped into the air, which was filled with the scent of fragrant wood. In the forest, Huck crept silently though the foliage, scanning the crowd for Tom. As Judge Thatcher passed him, he crouched down, not wanting to be seen.

"Excuse me, Judge." It was Aunt Polly. She looked worried. "I was wondering if you'd seen Tom."

"Why, no," the judge said. "Last time I saw him he was with Rebecca. They were chasing around at the back of the cave." He glanced around the meadow. "I thought they came out with everybody else, but I don't see them."

The sheriff came running up to the judge. He was out of breath and obviously frightened.

Judge Thatcher put his hand on the sheriff's shoulder. "What is it?" he asked. "What's wrong?"

"I was making my rounds in town when I seen the door to the tavern standing open. I went inside and there he was—Emmett—lying there deader than a mackerel . . . with a big knife hole in his back."

In the woods, Huck started with fear and had to grab onto a branch to keep himself from falling over.

"A knife, you say?" the judge asked.

"Yes, sir," the sheriff said. "Only one man can throw a knife like that."

At these words, Aunt Polly rushed forward and grabbed Judge Thatcher's arm. "Injun Joe! He's come back to take his revenge on Tom!" she cried.

Another wave of fear swept over Huck. This time, it wasn't fear for himself—it was fear for his friend.

Judge Thatcher was visibly shaken. "And if Becky's with him . . ." He turned to the sheriff. His voice took on a new urgency. "We must organize a search party."

As the judge, the sheriff, and Aunt Polly ran off to find volunteers, Huck looked anxiously in the direction of the cave entrance. He darted from the protective cover of the forest and raced toward its dark opening.

◆ ◆ ◆

Up on the mountain, Injun Joe lugged the sack

containing the pick and shovel to a secret entrance to the cave. He parted some bushes and disappeared.

Behind him, Huck sat in a tree, watching. Then he pulled out his knife and turned it over and over in his hand. Was he ready? If it came down to it, could he fight Injun Joe?

◆ ◆ ◆

Becky entered another cave, filled with stalactites and stalagmites. The light from her lantern gave them an eerie, otherworldly shine. "Look at this cave," Becky said. "It's even more beautiful."

"We call it Aladdin's Palace," Tom said offhandedly.

Becky glared at him.

He grinned, and then, to show off, he cupped his hands over his mouth and shouted. "Helloooooooo!"

His voice echoed through the cavern.

◆ ◆ ◆

Injun Joe lifted his head. That was the sound of a human voice. And one that somehow was familiar. Silently, he moved forward, a large candle in his hand. As he crept, the candle dripped globs of hot wax onto the tunnel floor.

◆ ◆ ◆

Tom and Becky were having a hollering contest. Their voices echoed and bounced off the cavern walls. Suddenly, a rumbling sound like thunder vibrated through the cavern. Tom frowned and fell silent, but Becky yelled again, even louder.

Tom grabbed her arm. "Stop, Becky!" he said urgently.

"You don't tell me what to do." She jerked away from him. "Hellooooo!"

"No, Becky—!" But Tom's cry came too late. Several boulders rumbled loose and crashed into the cavern. Just in time, Tom yanked Becky away from the path of the avalanche she had started.

◆ ◆ ◆

Outside the cave, Judge Thatcher stood at the head of an armed group of men carrying flaming torches.

"Gentlemen," he addressed them. "Injun Joe has come out from hiding, perhaps to take his revenge on Tom Sawyer. My daughter and Tom Sawyer are still in the caves. Be on your guard—Injun Joe has killed twice. I believe he would not hesitate to kill again."

Muff Potter stepped forward. "I'd like to lead ya, Judge."

The judge looked at him for a long moment. He was touched by Muff's offer. "Let's go," he said finally.

◆ ◆ ◆

Tom dug desperately at the pile of boulders that now blocked their way out of the cavern.

"Oh, Tom, it's no use, we're trapped," Becky cried.

"Don't you worry, Becky," Tom said bravely. "We'll find a way out." He held up his candle. A light breeze made it flicker.

"This way," he said.

They moved around a large outcropping of rocks where they found a small tunnel. The wind from it blew in their hair and extinguished Tom's candle. He took the lantern from Becky. Hand in hand, they entered the tunnel.

◆ ◆ ◆

As Muff led the search party into Satan's Cathedral, he saw a cloud of dust waft out of a connecting tunnel. "Oh, lordy," he cried.

"What's it mean?" Judge Thatcher asked.

"There's been a cave-in," Muff said grimly.

◆ ◆ ◆

Tom held Becky close as they crept through what seemed like a forest of stone. Just minutes before, they had been frightened by a terrifying face. It was only a shadow, but both of them were still afraid. Their hearts beat rapidly as they paused in front of a rocky ridge.

"This is all the light we've got," Becky said, pointing to the almost burned-out candle stub in the lantern. "When it goes out, it'll be dark forever."

"Don't worry, Becky." Tom tried to sound reassuring and confident. "Everything's gonna be just . . ."

His foot slipped. He looked down, then knelt. "Wax?" he said. "And it's warm?"

A stalagmite stump on the ridge behind them cracked and creaked. Slowly Becky and Tom turned to face it. The stalagmite turned toward them. Their eyes bulged with fear.

"Injun Joe!" Tom cried.

Injun Joe was caked with mud and slime. Only his eyes, with their expression of pure evil, seemed alive. "Tom Sawyer!" he shrieked, like a devil from hell.

Becky screamed. Tom turned to her. "Run, Becky! Run!"

Becky ran as fast as she could. Tom took off behind her.

Injun Joe jumped down from the ridge and followed the light from Tom's lantern. They were easy prey. He'd get them sooner or later—probably sooner.

◆ ◆ ◆

Tom and Becky ran as they had never run before, glancing back every now and then in terror at Injun Joe, who was steadily gaining on them. At one point, Injun Joe reached out and grabbed Tom's shoulder. Becky screamed, but Tom wrenched free and ran on.

There was a small opening in the cave up ahead. It was too small for Injun Joe to get through, but he and Becky could do it. Tom pulled her toward it. "Becky, in here!"

They dove in through the hole just as Injun Joe slammed into the rock behind them. He reached through with his hand and swiped at Tom, cursing and growling, but he couldn't touch them.

They crawled down the passage, rounded a corner, and crawled over something dry and bony.

Tom held up his lantern. It was a skeleton, with a rusty cutlass in one hand and the tattered remains of an eye patch over one eye.

◆ ◆ ◆

The search party emerged from the cave. Aunt Polly rushed forward to get the news. Judge Thatcher took her hands in his. "There's been a cave-in," he said somberly.

"Oh, no," Aunt Polly whispered.

"The children may be all right. Muff says there are other ways in and out."

Polly swayed a little on her feet. "If I lose him again, I don't know what I'll do."

fifteen

The Richest Boys in Town

In the cave, Tom tried to reassure Becky, who was shaken up at the sight of the skeleton. "It's all right, Becky. It's One-Eye Murrell."

He picked up the rusty cutlass and waved it in the air. "He must've been hiding here when the army came t'get him. Looks like he got lost here and slowly . . . died . . ."

Tom's voice trailed off. He shouldn't have said that to Becky. She was scared enough already. He held out his hand. "Come on." They moved further down the passage.

◆ ◆ ◆

The cutlass in one hand, Tom led Becky down another small, dark passageway. Up ahead was an opening into a larger chamber.

"This way, Becky!" he said excitedly.

Tom stopped just in time. He was on the edge of a chasm. It appeared to be a bottomless pit. He teetered there for a moment, then Becky seized his jacket and hauled him back to safety.

They clutched each other and fell back against the chamber wall. As Tom straightened up, he saw something carved in the wall nearby: a big Roman numeral II.

"Number Two!" he exclaimed.

He swung the lantern around. On the far wall was a large rock formation shaped like a cross. "Under the cross!"

Becky looked baffled. "What are you talking about?"

As Tom scanned the chamber, he noticed an incline leading up toward a small opening where the dawn sky peeked through. An exit! "Becky—look!" he cried.

She looked up. An expression of joy came over her face.

"Go on," Tom urged. "I'm right behind you."

But while she scrambled up the incline, Tom ran over to the cross instead. Just as he thought, there was freshly dug earth below his feet. He dropped to his knees and began to dig frantically with his rusty cutlass. In a moment, he had struck a hard object. It was Murrell's treasure.

"Tom!" Becky had reached the opening in the cave.

"Find your father!" he called back. "Bring him back!"

She hesitated, uneasy to leave him alone. "Tom?" she called again.

"Hurry!" he shouted.

Becky disappeared. Tom grabbed the chest and lifted it out. He pried open the lid and stared at all the gold and silver any boy had ever dreamed about. Suddenly, a vicious blow sent him sprawling.

"Looks like I get it all," Injun Joe said, looming over him with a malevolent grin. "The treasure and you."

He moved forward, pulling his long knife from his belt. Desperately, Tom swung the rusty cutlass into Injun Joe's leg. The man let out a cry of pain and staggered back.

Tom stumbled to his feet and charged Injun

Joe. But Joe was too good a fighter for him. With one easy punch, he knocked Tom to the ground again. The cutlass flew from Tom's hand and tumbled into the abyss.

With an evil smile, Injun Joe turned to Tom. Tom tried to run, but Joe pounced on him, seized him by the scruff of the neck, and raised his knife.

It was all over. Tom was going to die.

"Get your hands off my friend!" came a fierce—and familiar—voice.

Injun Joe turned in surprise. Huck Finn stood poised on the rocks above him. He launched himself into space and landed with both feet on Injun Joe's chest. Joe tumbled back, landing only an inch from the cliff's edge.

Not taking his eyes off Injun Joe, Huck helped Tom up.

"Huck . . ." Tom said in amazement.

Injun Joe leaped to his feet. His knife flashed in the lantern light. He stared at Huck. "I know you. You're Pap Finn's boy—Blueberry!"

Huck shot him a look of hatred. "Huckleberry."

"Your old man was the best knife-fighter on the Mississippi. Did he teach you?" Injun

Joe asked, advancing slowly on Huck.

Huck whipped out his knife. "He taught me."

"Then let's see what you got—river trash."

Huck's eyes narrowed in fury. "I ain't river trash."

The man and the boy dueled back and forth, moving closer and closer to the cliff's edge. Joe's knife slashed at Huck's tattered clothing, but Huck held his own.

"You got guts, boy," Injun Joe said, almost admiringly. "And in a minute, they're gonna be on the ground."

Joe feinted with his knife and landed a vicious and unexpected punch on Huck's jaw that sent the boy flying backward.

As Injun Joe raised his knife above a stunned Huck, Tom searched desperately for a weapon. There was only the chest of coins.

"It's over, boy," Joe hissed to Huck. "I never miss."

"Let's see you hit this!" Tom yelled from behind him.

Injun Joe whirled around. Tom was holding the treasure chest over the abyss.

"No!" Joe cried, forgetting about Huck. He charged Tom.

Tom's eyes widened with fear as Joe seized the treasure chest from him.

Suddenly the rock under Injun Joe's feet began to crumble. He tottered and tipped, then clutched desperately at Tom's sleeve with his free hand.

Tom cried out. Injun Joe was going to drag both of them to their death. But Huck grabbed Tom's other arm and tried to pull him back. For a moment, the three of them seesawed on the edge of the abyss.

With a ripping noise, Tom's jacket split at the shoulder. Injun Joe screamed wildly, then fell down into the pit, still clutching the treasure chest in one hand and Tom's sleeve in the other.

Tom and Huck fell back on the ledge, gasping for breath. It was over. Their worst, most fearsome enemy was gone.

"What made you come back?" Tom asked after a while.

Huck was silent for a moment. Then he simply said, "When a friend is in trouble, you don't run away."

◆ ◆ ◆

The two boys looked over the cliff's edge. "Well, I guess Injun Joe got his treasure," Huck said with a sigh.

"No, he didn't," Tom said.

Huck frowned. "What do you mean?"

"The chest—it was—I couldn't lift it," Tom said. His eyes sparkled. "It was too heavy. I had to tip most of the coins out . . ." He pointed to the place where Injun Joe had hit him. A pile of gold and silver coins gleamed in the darkness.

"Tom! Tom, are you down there?" It was the sheriff, peering down from the hole in the ceiling. Becky was at his side, a worried expression on her face.

At the sound of the sheriff's voice, Huck slipped back into the shadows, but before he could disappear, Tom seized his arm and hauled him forward.

"Who's that?" Becky asked.

"Becky, I'd like you to meet my friend Huckleberry Finn!" Tom announced proudly. "He just saved my life from Injun Joe. And he's one of the two richest boys in the county!"

Huck stared at Tom in surprise.

"Who's the other one?" the sheriff asked.

Tom grinned. "You're lookin' at him."

He stepped aside so that the sun illuminated the pile of shining coins. Gasps of astonishment came from Becky and the sheriff. Tom winked at Huck.

Huck broke into a huge grin. It was the first time Tom had ever seen him smile.

◆ ◆ ◆

Tom and Huck emerged from the cave carrying armloads of gold. The waiting crowd cheered wildly. Aunt Polly rushed to embrace Tom; Judge Thatcher shook his hand; he and Huck slapped each other on the back. And right in front of everyone, Becky rushed into Tom's arms and kissed him. It was much better than coming back from the dead.

"Young man!" The Widow Douglas addressed Huck. "What's to become of you? Have you begun to think about your future?"

"No, ma'am." Huck shook his head. "Never had one."

"Well, you've got one now and you'd best begin," she said crisply.

"Three cheers!" Muff cried out. "Three cheers for the bravest boys in Hannibal!"

◆ ◆ ◆

The newspaper headlines on the front page read: TOM SAWYER, HERO—BOYS DISCOVER LOST TREASURE.

All decked out in new clothes, scrubbed and shining, Tom smiled in satisfaction as he read the headlines. Then he sauntered down Main Street. People slapped him on the back, smiled, and congratulated him as he passed.

But catching sight of himself in a storefront window, Tom winced. Was that gussied-up kid really him? Suddenly he began to run. He shrugged out of his jacket, ripped off his collar and tie, and yanked off his boots and socks.

Barefoot, in only a shirt and pants, Tom began to run toward the hills.

◆ ◆ ◆

"Huck! Hey, Huck!" Tom yelled. He burst into Huck's home. But his friend was not there, only a well-dressed boy who was poking through Huck's belongings.

"Hey! Who are you?" Tom demanded. "What are you doin' here?"

"Takin' one last look. That okay with you?" The boy turned. It was Huck. A Huck with neatly combed and cut hair, a scrubbed face, and new clothes. He was almost unrecognizable.

"Huck?"

"What do you think?" Huck asked.

"I think one of us has lost his mind."

"The Widow Douglas is gonna adopt me," Huck announced.

"The Widow? Well, she's okay. But, Huck . . ." Tom indicated the camp. "You're givin' this up? Movin' to town?"

"Why not?"

"Why not!" Tom was indignant. "I'll tell you why not! Huck Finn goin' to church? Huck Finn goin' to school?"

"I start tomorrow mornin'," Huck said. He looked pleased.

"I gotta sit down," Tom said.

He lowered himself onto Huck's throne, shaking his head sadly. "Huck, you're the last person in the world I ever expected to get civilized."

"I done a lot of things, Tom, but I ain't never been civilized. I figure it'll be kind of an adventure."

Huck gave his home one last glance. "I gotta get goin'. Promised the Widow I'd take her to the church social."

"Church social?" Tom cried, aghast.

Huck nodded.

Something snapped in Tom. "That's it!" he

cried. "That tears it! You want to turn into a town boy, go ahead. I ain't gonna stop you! But I'm stayin' right here. I'm gonna live here in the open like a free man! And I ain't never goin' back! Somebody's gotta carry on!"

He folded his arms across his chest and scowled fiercely.

"Suit yourself, Tom," Huck said. "I hope it works out for you. Nights out here are awful cold sometimes." He turned to go. "If you change your mind, you know where to find me."

"And you know where to find me!" Tom shot back.

As Huck walked off through the trees and down toward Hannibal, a furious Tom watched him go. How could Huck abandon his free and idyllic life and go to live with the Widow Douglas? He was letting himself down, he was letting Tom down . . .

A cold wind whistled through the trees. Tom shivered.

"Huck!" he yelled suddenly. "Hey, Huck! Wait for me!"

"You comin' along?" Huck asked as Tom caught up with him.

"I guess I got to," Tom said. "Somebody's gotta look out for you. Civilization can be a dangerous place."

The two friends laughed together as they walked back to town.